MW01194199

The village of Styesville has a dragon problem, and is in sore need of a knight in shining armor to solve it for them. Instead, they get a strange traveler in a ragged cloak they barely even notice at first. Worse still, it soon becomes clear the problem setting fire to their village isn't as simple as a dragon...

The Faerie Godmother's Apprentice Wore Green
By Nicky Kyle

Edited by J. Ang
Cover designed by London Burden

Second Edition August 2019
First edition published by Less Than Three Press, LLC
Copyright © 2019 by Nicky Kyle
Printed in the United States of America

This story is for Sara Fox, who was kind enough to make me write it; for Mary Lou Roe, who led me into books; and for Kathy Kyle, who taught me the strength of princesses —and of dragons.

The Faerie Godmother's

apprentice

Wore Green

Nicky Kyle

The dragon came with the first new moon of spring. Everything was still wet, muddy, and half-frozen, which was what saved the village from burning down when the beast passed by overhead. It raked them twice that first visit, spouting a stream of blue-orange fire from its fanged jaws before banking out of sight over the forest. It left panic and soot in its wake. Those houses roofed in thatch were too damp to burn but it was three hours before the few buildings topped with pricier wooden shingles finally stopped smoldering.

Less than an hour after that, messages were heading with all possible haste to the surrounding towns to spread the word that Styesville had a dragon problem and shining knights were needed.

When help finally came, it wasn't the shining knight that was expected. There was no clanking armor, no noble steed, no razor-sharp sword of peerless steel. There was no unfurled banner, no shield with heraldic device, no panting squire trailing on a trusty pony. There wasn't even a lone knight-errant with dented helm and rusting chainmail plodding up the road on a boney, graying gelding. Instead there was just a shabby figure in a long patched cloak come walking into town on its own two feet. It bore a scarf wrapped thick against the damp evening chill, boots well-worn and trailing mud, and a much-mended pack that weighed its shoulders into a round stoop. Little wonder then that no one in Styesville noticed that help was here at last; little wonder that few noticed the traveler at all.

Ordinarily such a small, off-the-beaten-path village would have made much of any new arrival, even one so shabby, but these days they were focused more on their dragon than on gossip from distant places. Since the newcomer clearly had not come to rid them of their fire-breathing pest, being neither clanking nor shining nor even visibly armed, few of the villagers who had gathered in the smoky inn that evening paid the new arrival any mind, preferring to complain about their own winged problems over asking after whatever troubles might be plaguing any of their neighbors

Those complaints were punctuated by the sympathetic thumps of mugs and tankards and the occasional epithet spat contemptuously in the direction of the low fire smoldering in the hearth. Spring nights in Styesville were damp and chill, and Solm the innkeeper had learned long ago that people who were comfortable—or mayhap even a little over-warm—bought more drinks than people who were shivering. It was worth the effort of him chopping extra wood, or the expense of paying someone else to deliver fresh logs every day, for the increase of sales. Since it had yet to be burned down, the inn was one of the few places prospering under the dragon's eyes, although Solm was careful not to ever mention that fact and, indeed, took care to supply a free round of drinks every now and then as an expression of his sympathies toward the rest of Styesville. When the general griping about the dragon turned more personal as the evenings lengthened, both Solm and his wife, Myam, often took the precaution of retiring early before anyone could notice that trade at the small inn had more than doubled since the dragon's arrival. They did the same this night, and left their daughter in charge of serving the room while they excused themselves from the discussion. After a brief period of morose reflection, it was starting to get noisy again.

"I lost three goats yesterday—three!"

"Aye, but two of 'em had just run off on account of being afeared of the thing. Found them in my garden three hours later, didn't you?"

"That's not the point, and I paid you fair trade for all the tomatoes they trampled—"

"I'm just saying shingles is supposed to be *better* than thatch. It costs more don't it? It's not right when a person scrimps and saves to be able to afford the best only to have some—some big *lizard* come around and turn the edges into charcoal while them with thatch don't suffer more than a bit of smoke. It's not *fair*."

"Oh yes? And what are we going to do when summer comes 'round, eh? When everything's dry as tinder-boxes and a thatched-roof will go up in flame at the first hint of a spark? Bet we'll all wish we could afford shingles then."

"Surely we won't still be beset by this beast by summertime!"

"Do *you* see anyone come to help us? Face it, Jak, unless you've a princess or a duchess on hand to give away—or a glittery pile of gold at the least—knights have better places to waste their time and adventures than some dung-heap cluster of huts that can't muster more than a few sheep and some shillings for a reward. The dragon will grow bored with our ashes long before *we* see any knights come riding up that road to save us."

The miller's bitter statement was met by outraged protests but none that carried much conviction.

The stranger settled in at the corner of the room farthest away from the hearth and the cluster of disgruntled villagers sitting around it and rapped politely on the wooden counter to get the attention of the young woman cleaning mugs. She looked away from the discussion with a guilty start, her curls bouncing, then hurried over. "Good eve sir, begging your pardon! It's not often we get travelers here and sometimes I think that lot would just as soon serve theyselves and — well, what can I get for you?"

The stranger's heavy pack thumped against the wooden

floor as it was set down; something inside clanged metallically. "I'll take a mug of whatever you recommend, and a bit of supper, please."

The young serving-maid nodded amiably enough but her expression was dismayed. "I'm afraid your choices are ale or mead, nothing fancy, unless you want to try an early-press cider. As for supper, it's either stew or pie. We mostly serve bachelors what don't want to be troubled with cooking for themselves," she explained apologetically, "or a few of the old folks what would rather eat here than deal with all the grandkids underfoot at home, that sort of thing. We don't see a lot of *proper* visitors in these parts. Maybe a few deep-woods hunters or trappers or the odd wandering bard passing through on their way to more interesting parts now and again, but little else. There's not much need 'round here for fancy foods or diverse menu options and more's the pity about that, sir."

The stranger's hood hid everything but the prow of a long nose sticking out over that loose scarf like a ship's figurehead, but a chuckle emerged from the cloth-shrouded depths, followed by a question: "What's in the pie?"

"Potato," was the quick reply. "And cheese and herbs and spring onions. Some peas, but they was dried, so they don't add much taste — leastways not in my opinion they don't."

"I shall try the pie. And the cider. Thank you."

"Cider's strong," the serving-maid warned over her shoulder as she bustled away. The stranger grunted and turned to watch the loose circle of villagers. They were angry, their noisy complaints proved that much, but there was an undercurrent of fear in their voices too. They were afraid of the beast, afraid of what it had done already and what it would do next. Of course they were; dragons were dangerous, too dangerous for untrained villagers to fight.

Only knights specially schooled in the art of dragon-fighting stood a chance against the dreadsome beasts, and even they tended to come away from any conflict crisped and blistered more often than not, when they came away alive at all. Dragons were monsters, everyone knew that, some of the most dangerous monsters out there. There was a reason the rewards for dealing with the beasts were traditionally so large; there was a reason nobody sensible wanted to face one themselves and these villagers were no fools. They knew what they had hanging over their heads and their homes, and the fact that it had yet to do more than singe them didn't detract from their terror of what it could do when it chose to become more involved with their lives and livelihoods.

Aside from the newcomer, the only person in the room who wasn't trembling at least a little was the serving-maid. Her hands were steady as she carried a tray to the group of grumblers and refilled their tankards; steady as she poked up the fire smoldering in the hearth; steady as she brought food and drink over to the curious cloaked traveler.

"What is your name, mistress?"

"Louisa," the woman said. She was young and round, her chubby form just beginning to cross from coltish to coquettish. Her skin was the color and softness of a peach, scorched bright pink with an early sunburn across plump cheeks and an upturned nose, and her hair was a mass of curls the color and sheen of fresh honey. "Louisa Cooper, if it please you." She ducked a little curtsy as she placed the pie and tankard of cider on the long trestle table. "And you, er...mister?"

"Mistress," the stranger corrected her, but kindly. "Or simply Dea. I'm hardly a mistress, just a lone wanderer." Her voice was low and quiet, rough as though her throat was sore or perhaps as though she spent much of her time yelling; it offered no more hint of her gender than did the tall, narrow form swathed in thick fabric. Brown hands emerged from the rough - spun cloak she wore to wrap around her tankard and lift it to her mouth. She did not remove her scarf, but sipped carefully over the edge of the dark green wool. "Ah, you are right, that *is* strong. And quite fresh. Thank you."

Louisa blinked, then shrugged. "Well, if you like it, we've plenty. There's not many can stomach more than a glass or two, and most roundabouts here prefer ale."

"And you, Mistress Louisa?"

"Oh—ale's all right, or mead, although I'm not much for cider. Not the early stuff that's as strong as this, anyway." Louisa giggled and skipped back over to the grumbling crowd for a round of refills. The traveler called Dea watched her speculatively while she dug into her pie with the rough-forged iron fork that had come with the mug and the dish. It was a good pie, although the potatoes were a little overpowered by the strong, fresh onions. Still, it was hot and the crust was delightfully crisp, and it had been weeks since Dea had had a proper meal rather than something cooked haphazardly over a campfire, and she ate it hungrily. She pretended she didn't notice that Louisa kept looking over at her.

Dea was watching Louisa as well at any rate, although more subtly. (The deep hood and high scarf helped, as did the forkfuls of pie.) The serving-maid was a lovely girl, with the gold-twist curls and long-lashed eyes so common to tavern wenches in bardic songs. Her practical bodice and full skirts complimented her plump figure and, as one might expect of a tavern wench, did quite a good job of accenting her swell of a bosom too. The way her round cheeks puckered into friendly dimples when she smiled gave her features an inviting expression, but Dea noticed that none of the men-folk in the cluster of villagers around the fire seemed to pay her any undue attention; certainly there were none of the friendly pats to her behind or leering glances down her cleavage that one might expect to find in such a rustic setting. It was almost as if there was some sort of unwritten "hands off" rule about the girl, which would be an uncommon thing to find in a plain village inn like this one whose usual trade doubtless consisted mostly of bachelors, the occasional spinster, and those who preferred to spend as little time with their family as possible—just as Louisa had described. Perhaps her parents were strict and prudish and would withhold service from any fellow who gave their little girl too much sauce; if so they were less pragmatic than most innkeepers, to be willing to eschew good coin or barter over a bit of harassment.

Only one of the men there paid Louisa much notice beyond mumbling his thanks for a refill or scolding her for taking too long to bring one. He followed her with his eyes, blushing whenever she came near. He was a plain-featured fellow with pock-marked tan skin, hazel eyes, and floppy strawberry hair that could do with a trim. It looked like he was trying to grow a beard but wasn't having much success. He hadn't spoken yet that Dea had noticed, but instead sat quietly behind a portly man who shared enough of his looks that he was certainly a relative of some kind if not actually his father; Dea suspected he was the father from the way the boy glanced to him whenever he wasn't staring at Louisa. She smiled at the older man as readily as she did the rest of her customers, but when she served the boy she did it so fast his drink sloshed on the table and she didn't meet his eyes at all, for all that he never seemed to stop staring at her.

Dea rubbed her nose thoughtfully and returned her attention to her pie.

As she was finishing her meal Louisa came over to her again under the excuse of bringing a refill of cider, but once the drink was settled she sat down on the other side of the of the table and stared at the stranger. Dea kept eating, head down and shadowed under the depths of her hood. Louisa started to fidget, then to squirm, then finally to bounce. Eventually unable to hold her tongue any longer, she burst out, "You don't have to be afeared, you know."

Dea looked up. She put down her fork. "Of the dragon?" she asked, rough voice mild.

Louisa shook her head. "Of being, you know, *seen*." Flustered, blushing hard, she hurried to explain, "Oh, well, of course you should be afeared of the dragon. Although you don't come from here, so mayhap it won't have cause to hurt you, I don't know; we don't know why it came. Could be it's vengeance for something, in which case it'll leave you be, you not being from Styesville, or could be it's just hungry, in which case you're in as much danger as anyone although so far it's eaten naught but livestock." She cleared her throat and pressed on, at first haltingly and then in a breathless sort of hurry as the words ran away from her: "But what I meant, well, it must be warm in here under all that, and you don't need it. The cloak and the scarf and all. We've no magistrates around, and we certainly don't have the coin to attract bounty-chasers, so if you're hiding from the law or some lords you needn't worry. No one here would turn you in anyway," she added in a voice that warbled with uncertainty, "we aren't that sort of folk. Well, unless you'd done something terrible like horse-theft or murder." She giggled nervously. "And if you're a deserter from someone's army or service, well, everyone is entitled to their own choices and no one here will hold you to account for that. Besides, we haven't had any visitors pass through in weeks — not since the trouble started, so nobody here would have even heard about it if somebody *was* looking for you, so it's not like you'll be recognized anyway. Not that you look knavish anyway, I don't mean to imply you're done summat to be ashamed of! I don't mean to offend and maybe I have and I'm sorry if so, but I just didn't like the thought of you being uncomfortable 'cause you thought you had to hide, and if I've insulted you I didn't mean to and I'm sorry for it but you really can take your cloak off. If you want to."

Louisa swallowed hard and clammed-up all at once, like a river suddenly blocked by a rockslide, the tumbling rush of speech abruptly at an end. Her round face shone with concern and her pink cheeks darkened like ripening apples under Dea's gaze. Her bosom rose and fell like a fast tide; so many words so fast had left her gasping. As she slowly got her breath back she looked up through her lashes at Dea and cringed slightly, her expression one of tight worry.

When the only sound that came out of that worn hood was a low chuckle, Louisa sagged in relief. She went so limp that she nearly slid right off her stool and had to grasp the sides of the round seat to hold herself upright.

"I appreciate your concern," Dea said, "but you needn't worry that I have the law dogging my heels. I wasn't hiding my face because I feared being recognized, but because I did not want to startle anyone. If it upsets you so much to think of me overheating, though... " Slowly she unwrapped her scarf and pushed her hood back, revealing a face with strong, planar features, thin lips, and a broad beak of a nose. Her hair looked black in the dim light and it was cropped short in tight, ragged curls that were clustered untidily after so long under her hood. Her skin was the same rich brown as her hands, but—it wasn't all *skin*.

Louisa gasped, one hand flying to her mouth and the other clutching the edge of the stool still. Her eyes flickered back and forth across Dea's face, taking in the unmistakable sheen of green-tinged scales that were spread in patches across sharp cheekbones and down from a high forehead and crawling in like beads of greenish sweat at her square temples. A second, closer glance at those hands revealed more than a hint of scale around the knuckles as well. They had gone unnoticed in the murky light but perhaps they might have passed unseen even in the sun; the human mind is skilled at overlooking what it does not expect to see, and there are few who expect a splash of scales across a woman's face.

"I... I don't..." Louisa glanced at the cluster of grumbling villagers, but none of them were paying the two women any mind. In the dim light from the smoldering hearth-fire it was unlikely that anyone sitting farther away from Dea than Louisa was would notice anything out of the ordinary in the way the firelight glistened a little more on certain patches of Dea's skin or caught in the cracks between the shiny scales.

Dea smiled and said gently, "I'm not much afraid of that dragon, either."

Louisa blinked. Her hand trembled against her lips. "Did...did a dragon do that to you?" she asked, her voice a whisper of horror.

Dea hesitated. "Not exactly," she said. "In a way, I suppose. It's not much of a story, though. Perhaps you should tell me about *your* dragon, instead?"

Louisa bristled primly. "It's no dragon of *mine*."

"No, of course it isn't *yours*." Dea smiled an apology. "Just the dragon that has been causing problems around here lately, is all I meant. I'm quite curious. It's not often one finds a town plagued by dragon-raids in these parts, and I'm interested to know more about it. Could you tell me about it?"

Louisa flushed pink. "Oh," she said meekly, "of course. Well, there's not much to tell, really. It's a dragon; it's been doing the usual sort of thing. Carrying off a few sheep, some goats, once a couple of chicken but we found feathers and—and bones and flesh just a few yards outside of town, so that might have been a mistake. Mayhap chickens squirm more than sheep, or mayhap it's that dragons don't much care for the taste of other flying creatures, I don't know."

"Dragons aren't that picky about their food," Dea said drily, then waved for Louisa to continue when she paused to stare curiously.

"Well... it gives us a bit of a scorching every time it flies over, and a few people have been singed but nothing too bad, nothing worse than a bad sunburn and a bit of burnt hair really; most of the houses have been blistered more than once although nothing's caught on *proper* fire yet, not the sort that really burns—"

"I notice the inn here seems unscorched." Dea waved a hand around the dim-lit room.

"And a good thing, too," Louisa nodded. "All the casks and barrels in here, and all those years of spilled drink soaking into the floor, I shudder to think what would happen if the dragon turned its fire on this old place! Pa frets himself into a swivet every time we hear so much as a flap of wings, and ma fainted day before last even though it was just crows overhead. They—we—can't stop worrying it's going to come this way next time and light the place up like a torch. Half the village would probably go up with it if it did; there'd be no stopping such a fire once it got going, with all that alcohol to fuel it."

"Fortunate that the dragon hasn't turned its attention this way then," said Dea, her voice bland.

"Very fortunate. It hasn't done much damage at all really," Louisa said with a shrug. "I suppose we've all been fortunate so far, although you wouldn't know it the way *some* complain. Summer's coming on soon though, and then things will start getting dry and it'll be a fair bit more dangerous than it is now, having a big scaly beastie flying around spitting sparks over our heads. We're all hoping that a knight will turn up afore then but it seems, if folk are thinking about it right," she jerked her head at the crowd of complainers around the hearth, "that we haven't got very much to entice one with, so perhaps that's unlikely." Louisa sighed dramatically and propped her chin on her hand, the picture of beleaguered misery in full commiseration with the rest of the crowd. It seemed more play-acted than anything else though, a child dressing-up in a borrowed attitude and pa's old boots that were much too big not to trip over.

Dea rubbed her chin. "I imagine most of the village's attention is on the dragon right now," she said slowly. Louisa nodded. "Lots of other things, the usual traditions and gatherings and so forth, are all being put on hold while it's out there, am I right?"

"Oh yes," said Louisa. "Nobody's much in the mood to think of anything else aside from the dragon, are they?"

"So none of the regular village festivals or celebrations— seasonal events, age-rights, weddings, all those sorts of things that punctuate regular life—I mean, how could you even think of making the effort of arranging a festival when you never know when a great fiery lizard might descend from the sky and ignite everything in sight? I'm sure that's what everybody's been saying about it."

Louisa shook her head. Her eyes flickered to the hearth and back again. "That's right, miss. Seems like it would be bad form too, celebrating much of anything when there's a dragon in the woods."

"No doubt." Dea drummed her fingers on the table. Her

nails were thick, heavy things: a dark greenish-black color that contrasted sharply with her warm brown skin. The color made it look like she had been digging in some particularly putrid swamp and hadn't had a chance to clean-off yet, but they were more solid than human nails generally grew; more like claws than nails really. They made a hollow, heavy clicking sound against the wood that sent a shiver up Louisa's spine. "Well, I suppose the only thing to do is go and look around for myself."

"What?" Louisa scrambled to her feet when the taller woman stood up and stretched, arms over her head and back crackling.

"The dragon," Dea asked absently, rolling her neck across her shoulders, "does it only come during the day, or does it sometimes come at night?"

"Only during the day," Louisa answered, her voice faint. "So far."

"Shouldn't be any danger then," Dea said, adjusting her cloak and straightening her short brown tunic. "You'll look after my things for me?" she asked, jerking her chin toward the sagging pack that rested against her abandoned chair.

Louisa nodded but she didn't look happy, and not about having to be responsible for the other woman's possessions. "Miss, you can't—you can't be thinking of going to look for the *dragon*, can you?"

"Didn't I say to call me Dea?"

Louisa gave no reply but mutely raised glistening wet eyes in an unmistakable plea. Dea sighed, her own eyes lifting toward the skies beyond the inn's roof as if searching for empathy from some distant, airborne creature. "Oh, don't fret so. Of course I'm not going to look for the *dragon*. I just want to peek around, see what sort of damage it's done to the town, that sort of thing. And it'll be dark soon, so I'd best not wait too long."

"Miss—it's dark already, though," Louisa protested. "Why not take a room here tonight, look around tomorrow? We've very low rates and if you've not got the coin for it, ma is always happy to take barter for other goods, or you can exchange chores for board. We can always use an extra hand..."

"It isn't *dark*-dark," said Dea, as if she hadn't heard Louisa's offer. "More just...*dim*. And I have excellent night-vision besides." Before she flipped her hood back up the firelight caught her eyes at just such an angle as to make them look uncannily like a cat's: slit-pupiled and green. Louisa looked away. When she looked back Dea was wrapping her scarf around her face again, hiding that scale-pocked face from view. "No need to worry about me," Dea said, and patted the unhappy serving-maid reassuringly on the shoulder.

The griping cluster of villagers were so caught-up in their escalating complaints that they hardly noticed as Dea walked past them out the door and into the twilight lurking outside. She could hear their muffled calls for refills as the door swung shut behind her.

Several minutes of brisk exploration revealed that the village of Styesville would be quite prosperous if one held mud to be of great monetary value. Aside from that it boasted several scruffy goats, two herds of soon-to-be-sheared sheep, one rather elderly cow, and rather too many chickens to count. From the noises there seemed to be at least three pens that held pigs too but to the naked eye they appeared only to contain more mud, albeit mud that snuffled and snored and sometimes snorted. Dea smiled; she had always had a soft spot for pigs, who seemed so secure in themselves despite the crude and uncomplimentary things people so often said about the bristly beasts.

The mill at the edge of town held little interest for all that it seemed more prosperous than the rest of the town. A few black soot marks showed that it had been paid some attention by passing flame but not enough to crisp its precise wooden shingles or blacken its waterwheel, possibly because anything so close to a stream in muggy spring weather tended to develop a certain dampness that would have been of great annoyance to a dragon trying to ignite its soggy wood, or possibly merely because the rich often possess an uncanny luck for avoiding whatever troubles were plaguing their neighbors. While the miller of such a place as Styesville could not be a wealthy man, everything was relative—especially coin—and by the standards of the small village the miller was decidedly better off than most everyone else in town. Dea had no sympathy for the cosmetic damage he had suffered, though she told herself she ought to since it was neither the miller's fault that a dragon had come to town, nor that his profession was a lucrative one.

The rest of the buildings had all been treated to a bit more attention than had the mill, but only a bit; the inn itself had been, as Dea had noticed on her arrival, miraculously spared but everywhere else she saw signs of blackened thatch and charcoaled shingles. The rest of the town consisted of fewer than thirty wooden buildings, most of them small and no more than one story in height with perhaps enough room for an attic loft under the thick, damp thatch. Being surrounded by a dense forest, wood was a cheap and readily-available material and everyone had built out of it. Only the blacksmith's forge incorporated stone as befitted a building that was used to having fire around, although that fire tended to come from the heart of the forge rather than from overhead and there was little to protect its wooden walls or shingled roof from an errant blaze. If a dragon visited the forge in earnest, the blacksmith's home would burn as readily as everything else in Styesville.

Most of the brush, trees, and grass in the town sported crispy black evidence of flame-kisses along its upper leaves and branches but oddly none of the crop-fields or orchards around the village looked like they had suffered from so much as a whiff of smoke. Dea kicked a prickly patch of nettles on the side of the rutted dirt road; a small cloud of ash rose, but the plants themselves sprang back into shape with the ease of leaves that were healthy and well-watered.

There were buckets, jugs, and barrels sitting everywhere through the town; those seemed to be a recent addition and most already held precautionary water. Dea wrinkled her nose, thinking of the copious breeding-grounds so much standing liquid would offer for insects in the summer.

She knew that peasants were not traditionally educated in matters of hygiene and it was not their fault if they were ignorant of the dangers posed by stagnant water, but even a few decades of travel had not erased entirely her disgust for such unclean habits, for all that she had grown almost accustomed to the lice and fleas that were one's customary companions in the beds-for-rent found on the road. (It helped that her cooler-than-normal body temperature held little attraction for such pests.) Still, she was glad that she would be far away from here by summer and, if things went as she hoped, the villagers wouldn't have any need to keep such unhygienic fire-prevention around by then and would thus be spared the inevitable insect infestation as well as the illnesses that so often resulted from such welts and swellings. She resisted the urge to kick the buckets over; even if she had explained the risk to the villagers they would doubtless prefer the threat of disease to the danger of being burned alive.

Dea walked to the town well, which at least had a sturdy wooden cover over it. There was a multitude of precariously-stacked vessels clustered around the circle of stone although those were mercifully empty. She skirted them with ease; the piles of crockery had been laid-out with wide paths between them, as though to allow a great number of people to run to the well without fear or tripping or trampling. The inhabitants of Styesville were a people well-prepared for ravaging flames for all that they had been but lightly-scorched so far.

It was all very interesting but not particularly surprising, Dea thought as she walked out toward the edge of town. It never did to act on assumptions though, and she wanted more evidence before she would let herself come to any conclusion, no matter how obvious the situation seemed at first glance. Even now there was one more thing yet she had to check before she could be sure she'd guessed right. And this particular guess would be an awful one to get wrong; Dea liked dragons, and would hate to be savaged by one by accident. She had to find *proof* of her supposition.

As she had told Louisa she did indeed have excellent night-vision and the haze of thickening twilight did little to hamper her investigation of Styesville, but in the end it was her nose that led her to what she sought.

Most folk walking down the dirt track that led from the village-center into the southern forest would never have noticed it—had in fact not noticed it for some days now, according to the stink—even if they had been looking (or sniffing) for it, as Dea was. While her nose wasn't nearly as acute as her eyes it was still a sensitive nose, and growing longer every day. Besides, the smell of carrion was unmistakable to someone who had spent so much time traveling alone on the road in places often inhabited by either hungry bandits, hungry animals, or both. There was nothing like the scent of meat rotting in the sun to warn a person to be on their guard, or maybe find a different path to take altogether.

This time rather than avoiding the stink Dea followed her nose back to the sickly-sweet source of the smell. When she left the road and headed into the field beside it she took as much care as she could not to crush the tender spring shoots of new wheat clawing their way through the damp earth, out of consideration for whatever nervous farmer was doubtless already fretting over his fragile harvest under the eye of an unpredictable dragon. She still left a trail of battered stalks behind her, clear evidence that nothing else had passed this way recently—nothing moving on foot, anyway, since hers was the only path of bent and broken stalks in the whole of the rippling, knee-high field.

Then she came to the blood-splattered hole of broken, flattened crops. They circled the thing she had smelled from the road. It had burst when it hit the ground and two or three days in spring sunshine and dampness had not improved its condition so it was hard to tell what species it had been originally, but there was enough red-dyed wool mixed amongst the rotting flesh and splintered bones that she was reasonably sure that she was looking at something that had once been a sheep—maybe two sheep even, but certainly no more than three; there wasn't enough meat for more than that even taking into account that much of it had been nibbled by carrion-feeders by now. Dea searched for a few minutes before she gave up on finding a stick, or a stalk firm enough to use like one, and poked the carcass gingerly with the toe of her boot instead. It went *plorp* and released a fresh bubble of noxious stink that made her gag; a number of buzzing insects rose angrily from the bloated flesh to protest the disturbance and the short, plump coils of maggots growing and gorging in the meat writhed in a fashion that caused unpleasant feelings in the pit of her own well-fed stomach.

Five fat crows that had been startled into flight by her arrival now watched her reproachfully from their seats around the edge of the unbroken stalks. Dea couldn't speak crow but she could recognize insults in a number of human languages and crow-epithets tended to be even more vulgar and pointed so she had little doubt that what they were saying about her interrupting their dinner was unkind. She gave the birds a polite little bow and returned to the road, considerately picking her way gingerly back along the same footprints she had left on her way into the field. She didn't bother to look up at the sky where the night's first stars were starting to flicker. Now that she had spoken to Louisa and seen the rest of the village, and those trembling villagers, and found that sad splattered carcass, she had a pretty good idea of what she was dealing with and she was no longer even a little bit concerned about the dragon.

Most of the inn's other guests had left by the time she returned; it was proper-dark outside now and Louisa was going around cleaning up the mugs and plates and bits of food left behind by the evening's trade. She was a dutiful girl, probably the sort who made her parents proud in a bemused and distant sort of way—the sort of girl of whom people would say, "she'll make a good wife for someone someday," as if that was a compliment. Dea almost grimaced. She had probably received a number of politely-muttered "good eve's" and "pleasant night's" from the grumbling crowd as she had shown them out and she had probably had a cheery smile for every one of them in return.

None of the complainers were left now, although the two women weren't quite alone in the inn yet. One shriveled old man sat snoring noisily in a corner chair and two others of advancing age and receding hair sat bent over half-full tankards and a shabby checkers set at a table placed close enough to the fire to give them light but far enough away that their game would not have been disturbed by the evening's discussion of dragon-trouble. A handsome woman whose heavy muscles and soot-streaked clothes proclaimed her to be the blacksmith was counting out coppers on the table. Louisa stood next to her trying not to look like she was watching to double-check the amount. They both looked up when Dea opened the door, Louisa with a nervous smile that radiated relief like post-rainstorm sunlight and the older woman with politely disinterested curiosity.

Dea nodded amiably and retreated to her former seat at the far end of the room as the blacksmith left, her tab paid. Louisa lost no time in putting down her cleaning rag and tray of dirty mugs and rushing over. Dea was still unwrapping her scarf when the girl skidded to a stop next to the table, hands white-knuckled where she braced them on its edge.

"You're all right? You didn't meet the dragon?"

Instead of answering Dea shook her head and asked a question of her own. "When are you getting married?"

Louisa recoiled as though slapped. "When am I what?"

"Your wedding," Dea repeated amiably, "when is it?"

"I—it—we're not sure." Her eyes darted around the room, looking at everything except for Dea. "What with the dragon in town, anything like that has been delayed..."

"Ah yes, you said that earlier. Sensible decision," said Dea. "How long has the dragon been visiting?"

"Been almost two months now."

"So it showed up just after the marriage was arranged, then?"

Louisa's jaw dropped. "How could you know that?"

"I guessed," Dea said. "Would you sit down with me for a little?"

"Oh." Louisa's cheeks flushed pink. "Of course." She followed her over to one of the tables near the fire, away from the chess players. Dea pushed back her hood, exposing those gleaming scales and cat-pupiled eyes again, and her close-cropped tuft of dark hair.

She took Louisa's hands between her own, making the younger woman blush darker. "I want to tell you a story now. It's about a girl who once upon a time did not want to get married. She was a princess named Aldeaim—"

"Oh," Louisa said, dragging her eyes away from the clasped hands on the table, "I know that story. My granddam used to tell it to me when I was little. I always liked it, but I liked the one about Princess Gella more because it has a happy ending, and also the one about Princess Thaiyn who overthrew the wicked—"

"Hush," said Dea. "Let me tell the tale as I know it, all right?" She closed her eyes a moment, then cleared her throat and began. "Once upon a time, there was a princess who would not marry. Her parents tried everything: they hosted grand balls and athletic contests, held poetry readings, gathered scholars to debate literature and history, even offered a reward to any who could win their princess's heart, male or female or otherwise. When none of that worked they summoned wizards and wise-women to see if there was a curse on the girl but neither magic nor science could solve the problem; she simply wasn't interested in falling in love with anyone.

"At last, having no choice—because in their lands, no one could claim the throne alone you see, so even if Aldeaim had adopted an heir she would not have been allowed to rule without first choosing a consort—they penned the princess up in a tower and said that whoever could overcome the enchantments and guards they set around it would have her hand in marriage whether she liked it or not."

Dea smiled crookedly. "They thought, you see, that since all else had failed they might as well fall back on the oldest traditions and determine that whoever was worthy of their daughter—he or she or otherwise—would be able to breach the defenses and rescue her. They thought their daughter must be under a curse of some sort, no matter what the scholars and sorcerers said, because why else had she not fallen in love with *anyone* they had presented to her? They thought perhaps 'true love's kiss' would work to breach her heart where all else had failed, overcome the curse and save their daughter from a life alone and their kingdom from an empty throne."

Louisa was silent now, her lower lip caught absently between her teeth while she listened, a well-trained audience for a storyteller; Dea was no professional bard but she had done enough traveling that she was practiced at telling stories. Any newcomer in a small town could earn themselves a bit of supper by sharing news and gossip and, when those ran out, simply by telling tales that had not yet been told in that town.

She continued with a shrug. "Well, Princess Aldeaim was no keener on the idea of marriage now that she was in her tower than she had been before they locked her away, so she took desperate measures of her own. They had put quite a lot of books up there with her, you see, her parents; they did not want their princess to be bored while she waited. It wasn't that they were unkind, the queen and king, they simply thought they knew what was best for their daughter better than she did. It's quite a common state of parenting, isn't it?" She didn't wait for an answer, but Louisa squirmed uncomfortably before she went on. "Well, so they kindly left her with many diversions before they sealed the doors and summoned the brambles and monsters, and

Aldeaim had spent a lot of her time locked up in there reading. Some of the books were more useful than others, and one taught her some of the long-lost secrets of faerie godmothers."

"But those are just a myth," Louisa burst out, unable to stop herself interrupting. "Just a story folk tell girls to make them behave when they otherwise might not, because they think that as long as no faerie godmother has showed up to help then no matter how much they don't like what's going on, it can't be *that* bad or one *would*." She gulped then and sucked her lips in quick, as if she could take back the words. She started to stammer an apology but a gentle squeeze of her hands silenced her.

Dea smiled. "Not a myth in the way you might think. The truth has become quite obscured by mythology, yes—but the underlying idea remains true. We've simply grown confused about how it works. Faerie godmothers are indeed real; they are not, however, actually *faeries*. Well," she explained wryly, "faeries are fickle and capricious creatures, selfish and fond of pranks; they would obviously make terrible help-mates for a person in trouble. Who would want to call a *faerie* godmother to help them? It would only make things that much worse, getting a faerie involved. Dragons, on the other hand..."

Louisa's eyes were wide and fixed on Dea as if she could absorb the older woman's secrets just by staring at her. Dea pretended not to notice the desperate, hungry look in Louisa's eyes and continued:

"Dragons are reliable and constant. They have a strongly-developed concept of honor. They are also insatiably curious, and they love an underdog." Her teeth flashed in a grin. "They have an innate understanding of magical currents and very long life-spans, and they hate being bored. What better creature to invite to meddle in your life when you need help? Thus what Princess Aldeaim actually contacted, when she called for help from a faerie godmother, was a dragon—not a surprise to her, since she had read the whole book through and knew where the myth of faerie godmothers *really* came from; knew from the start that she was calling a dragon."

Dea's eyes were distant now, as if she looked through the fire smoldering in the hearth and out the other side to something else. "A great crimson beast with black claws and golden teeth and bright green eyes that glowed like a cat's in moonlight, wings as wide as the sky and softer and stronger than silk, a long tail like a drop-spindle unrolling..." She sighed, shook her head, and focused on Louisa again. "Well, at any rate the princess did not have to marry anyone because she flew away on dragonback—not kidnapped as the stories say, but because that's what she wanted to do and the dragon was kind enough to oblige when she explained the situation that had landed her at the top of that tower."

Louisa frowned. "She *wanted* to go with the dragon?"

"Most do, those whom folk say have been 'kidnapped.' Dragons have little interest in humans as captives. Well, they like people because of the stories they can tell and the trouble they can cause and the interesting ideas they have. Why would they want one who just sits around moping or wailing to go back home?" Dea shook her head. "That would be boring, and dragons *hate* being bored. No, they find it a lot more interesting to help people than trying to hurt them.

"Usually if a dragon is hindering someone," she explained, "it's to the benefit of someone *else* who asked them nicely. Or admittedly because they've decided to spread rumors of a treasure hoard so they'll always have company, which is a favored tactic of those too elderly to enjoy traveling anymore and who would rather have the world come to them, even if it comes with silly little sword in hand..." Dea chuckled, then frowned. "Sorry, now I'm getting off track. Anyway the point I was trying to make is that faerie godmothers *are* real, and they're dragons."

Louisa didn't look comfortable with that idea. "How can you be sure?" she asked.

Dea met her eyes. "Because I was saved by one, and now I'm becoming one."

Louisa looked very much like a milky-pink fish with her mouth hanging slack like that. Dea kindly made no mention of it.

"Once upon a time my name was Aldeaim and after I flew away, I decided that being a faerie godmother sounded like a much better life than being a princess, so I stayed with the dragon and studied her magical arts as her apprentice. Now I'm an 'apprentice faerie godmother' myself, for lack of a better term, and I travel to gain practical experience and help out where I can while I'm on my way to mastering my wings."

"That's impossible." Louisa was whispering now. "That was...the story of the beautiful-but-ice-hearted Princess Aldeaim happened over a hundred years ago."

Dea nodded. "Dragons live for a very long time. And it takes a *very* long time to become a dragon."

"But...but...people can't just turn into dragons!"

"Look at your hands. At *my* hands. You can see the scales—hellfire Louisa, you can *feel* them."

Louisa rubbed her thumb lightly across Dea's knuckles and the patches of scale growing through the skin. "Does it hurt?" she asked in a soft voice.

"No. Itches a bit, around the edges, sort of like—have you ever gotten a sunburn? I don't mean that little pink kiss across your cheeks, but a proper summer sunburn, the kind that peels." When Louisa nodded Dea said, "It's a bit like that, when the skin gets dry and curls off. That's how it happens around the scales: they grow up through the skin which flakes off around them. But it doesn't hurt."

"And that's going to happen... everywhere?"

"Oh yes," said Dea. "That's just the beginning too. The bigger changes come later, where the bones shift and I grow new teeth, and a tail and wings... and of course I'll get much, much bigger, too!"

Louisa shuddered. "I don't believe it. People *can't* turn into dragons. And what would the dragons say? They can't possibly *want* that to happen. What do *real* dragons think about it?"

"I'm going to *be* a 'real' dragon," Dea explained patiently. "Where do you think dragons come from? Eggs?" She snorted when Louisa nodded hesitantly. "Even leaving aside for a moment the fact that dragons don't have a sex and adopt a gender only out of curiosity or comfort, can you truly picture a great, massive creature like a dragon hatching out of an egg? Or brooding a clutch of them, for that matter? Let alone talk about mating and all the difficulties that would cause... " She shook her head. "Dragons like to socialize, yes, but only in small doses. Besides, most areas can only support one or maybe two dragons comfortably; they're too much of a strain on local resources in groups, so a whole nest... well! It wouldn't end well for anyone, I'm sure."

Louisa frowned. "Then where do they come from?" she asked.

"People, always people. Sometimes dragons are folk who've studied too much forgotten magical lore to enjoy being people anymore. Mostly though they used to be princesses—or princes. Sometimes a duchess or an earl. They're not always royal or noble, of course. I knew one, a beautiful grey-blue scaled creature with a voice like a thunderstorm, who used to be a merchant's daughter before she grew her wings. Most dragons were human nobility though, once upon a time."

At Louisa's expression of disbelief Dea said primly, "A royal education actually prepares one quite well for dragon-hood, believe it or not. It cultivates the right mind-set: a self-confident superiority coupled with a desire to meddle in other people's lives for their own good. Condescending, distantly affectionate, and curious—that's a good description of most dragons *and* of most of those kings and queens who actually do good things for their subjects. With such an overlap of personality, is it any wonder that dragons prefer to draw their next generation from noble human houses?"

Louisa didn't seem to realize that she was slowly shaking her head back and forth, her face slack. Dea smiled gently. "It's all right," she said. "It's a lot to take in. I had months to get used to the idea, reading up there all alone in my tower, and it was still a bit of a shock when I grew my first scale."

"So you're saying... you're saying that a princess summoned *this* dragon?" Louisa grasped at the question like a drowning woman clutching a bit of driftwood; grabbing the here-and-now because the way-back-then was too big to contemplate.

"I'm saying that's not a dragon at all. It's just the *idea* of a dragon—and it wasn't summoned by a princess, but rather by the daughter of an innkeeper."

"But I don't have any sisters, and there's not another inn around for miles and miles! What's it doing here?"

Dea said nothing but her gaze didn't waver. She continued to smile.

Louisa paled. "That's not—I didn't summon no dragon, you're mad!"

"You didn't mean to, which is why you didn't get a

proper dragon, an *actual* dragon," Dea explained, not unkindly. "You just got the *idea* of a dragon. It can't manage much flame and it fades out of existence when it gets too far away from you, which is why—I don't know if you've noticed, but everyone will if the 'dragon' is still here by summer when dead things start really stinking—if you go looking around beyond the village limits, you'll find all the bloody bits of what it stole to 'eat' splattered all over the ground. They fell when it dematerialized, I presume."

"I never... I couldn't... I didn't..."

"The marriage your parents arranged for you, it's to that boy who was watching you tonight?" Dea guessed. "Which is problematic, I assume, because you prefer women?" The bright flush that rose in Louisa's cheeks was answer enough.

"Well I can offer you a way out of your arrangement that doesn't require illusory dragons *or* carry a risk of burning down the whole village if things get out of control, if you'd like, although I'm afraid it isn't the escape you've been daydreaming about. I've no more interest in marriage now than I did when I went by my full name," she said, her smile wry but her rough voice as gentle as she could make it. Dragons can see into people's hearts and while Dea was as of yet no dragon, her eyes were by now less human than draconian and some things were easy to see even with a mortal gaze if one bothered to look. "I won't spirit you off for a runaway elopement, or challenge that young fellow to a fight for your hand, or overwhelm your parents with a bride-price of dragon gold—"

Astrangled sort of croak escaped Louisa's lips; she looked horrified. Dea squeezed her hands gently and added, "But I can take you away with me, if you want— as friends, perhaps, or at least as travel companions for a while." She smiled and extricated her fingers from Louisa's vise-tight grip. She didn't resist but she did drop her eyes to the floor.

They glistened wetly in the light of the dying hearth-fire.

Dea wasn't done speaking yet. "Anybody who can conjure a full-fledged projection of a dragon strong enough to actually scorch damp thatch and carry off livestock without any proper training is somebody who can do a lot more with her life than serve drinks and clean up spills. There's a university I know of that would be glad to have somebody of your natural ability. I'm not much for company on the road generally, but I think I could manage not to bite long enough to help you get there, if you'd like. And if not, there are plenty of places where a cheerful girl who knows how to balance a tray of drinks can make a living outside of Styesville and away from any well-intentioned meddlers with an interest in matrimony."

Louisa sat looking down at the table and her empty hands. After a while she said, in the sort of tightly-controlled voice that people use when they're trying to sound like they're more interested in rational logistics than anything as wet and untidy as emotions, "I haven't the coin to go to a fancy school. Even my dowry won't pay for something like that, providing I could somehow talk ma and pa into letting me spend it on learning instead of marriage, and I've no money of my own."

"I don't think you'll have to pay them a thing. The University of Alchemical Light has provisions for people of prodigious talents and modest backgrounds. I imagine they'll cover your costs and even give you a stipend for whatever their room-and-board arrangement doesn't provide in exchange for you agreeing to help instruct some of the lower classes when you move on to your higher levels of study; they've done that before. The current dean was herself one of their 'stipend students' when she studied there—if I've not lost track of time. They might have a new university head by now," Dea admitted. "I'm still getting used to measuring years in dragon-cycles."

They had both of them forgotten about the other people in the room, so it came as a surprise when a hoarse voice said, "This person botherin' you, Louisa?"

The women looked up to find the two grizzled game-players standing by their table. Neither looked happy. One stood with his arms folded across his chest, ropey muscles taut beneath skin so leathered by sun and weather that it was impossible to tell what color it had started as. The top of his head was completely bald but the rest of his hair seemed keen to make up for that lack, especially the bushy gray eyebrows that loomed like furious cocoons over his dark eyes. The other was shorter but broader, his muscles given over mostly to flab now but in the stretchy sort of way that showed there was still some iron hidden under the plump padding. His dark skin was marked with heavy freckles scattered across his cheeks like spattered ink and his coarse white hair stood out around his head like a pale nimbus, the light of the fire behind him making it almost appear to glow.

If neither was intimidating to a woman accustomed to walking through bandit country and facing-down unscrupulous toll-collectors and city guards with nothing but a toothy smile and a few magic tricks, they still tried to indicate that anybody giving Louisa any trouble would soon have trouble of their own from *them*, perhaps more than they looked likely to give at first glance.

Dea had to duck her head to hide a smile. She had a soft spot for protective but misguided old men; they always reminded her of that marvelous dragon.

Louisa was shaking her head vehemently, her honey-curls bouncing. "Oh no! No, thank you Gaffer Haush, Master Sellbick, no I'm not being bothered at all!"

Neither man looked convinced. Dea was careful to keep

her head down, momentarily lamenting the fact that she kept her hair cropped so short; longer locks would have served as something of a curtain to hide the scales on her cheeks. As it was she just had to hope that the men's eyes were rheumy and weak, or that they were old enough—and pragmatic enough—not to bat an eyelash at the sight of a few scales on a woman's face.

The silence stretched out and thickened, like yeast ripening a loaf of bread. Eventually the old man who had spoken said, "You looked a bit bothered." The belligerence was gone from his tone; he was just making conversation now although it was the sort of conversation that took care to indicate that, in the right circumstance, it could very quickly become belligerent again.

"No, no," Louisa fluttered her hands nervously. "No, I was just—the lady was telling me a story, that was all, and it wasn't a happy one. You've heard stories like that, the kind that don't have happy endings, yes?"

The old men exchanged a look. "Heard 'em once or twice," the darker one said drily. The bald one snorted and rubbed gnarled fingers swollen by arthritis across his chin with a sandpaper rasp. "Once or twice," he repeated.

"Mistress Dea was just telling me an old tale," Louisa explained, her voice hearty with forced cheer, "and I had forgotten how—how *sad* it is, that the girl in it had to leave, er, when the dragon carried her away, and how she never saw her parents again and nobody ever managed to find her and bring her home and, well we were talking about *our* dragon, and Mistress Dea wanted to know if it had carried any young ladies off and I said of course it hadn't, it's not as though we've any princesses in these parts after all, so what would a dragon want with anyone around here?"

"Might want the eatin'," muttered the man who had spoken first.

His companion elbowed him in his skinny ribs. "Don't scare the lass, Sam."

"Got a dragon flappin' around, don't need me jawin' to make folk afraid..."

Louisa raised her voice over their bickering. "It is quite sweet of you to be concerned for me, thank you, but I really am fine. It was just the story upset me, 'twas all."

"What story is that, now?"

"The one about Princess Aldeaim. You've heard it, I'm sure."

The old men exchanged shrugs. "Can't say as I recall it," said the first speaker, the one his friend had called Sam.

"Give an old man a hint eh, there's a girl," said the other man. "The old memory don't be so sharp as it once was."

Louisa glanced at Dea, who was studiously examining the table and doing nothing that would draw any attention her way. She didn't appear to care much about Louisa's conversation with Gaffer Haush and Master Sellbick. Louisa hesitated a moment, then said with deliberate cheer, "Well, it's that one about the princess who was so beautiful that everyone who met her fell in love right on the spot, only she had been cursed by a jealous sorceress who froze her heart—poor thing—so she could never, ever fall in love back."

She carefully did not look at Dea as she rushed on to add, "Well the sorceress locked her in a tower and put a hundred beasts around it to guard her and planted thorns that grew as tall as oak trees all around it, because she knew there was a brave prince who was in love with Princess Aldeaim who wanted to break the spell with a kiss of true love and she wanted to stop him of course, only he fought all the monsters and cut down all the thorns so when it looked like he was going to get into the tower and rescue the princess anyway the sorceress sent a dragon to carry

Princess Aldeaim away.

"That's how the story goes anyway," Louisa finished with a defiant little mutter, "although sometimes folk say it was the sorceress who turned *herself* into a dragon..."

"Lovely story, lass." The freckle-faced man patted her warmly on her shoulder while Sam nodded.

Louisa sniffled a moment, then smiled again and briskly changed the subject. "Well! It's far too late in the evening to start storytelling now anyway! Can I fetch another drink for either of you fellows?"

The bald man opened his mouth but the other one elbowed him in the ribs again. "Seein' as it's gettin' so late, methinks we'll be headin' on home now, lass. Been a fine evening, no sense dragging it out too long, eh? Just suffer for that in the morning, eh?"

"That's exactly right, Master Sellbick." Louisa nodded firmly and, with a combination of chatter and compliments, managed to chivvy them both out the door. Before it shut the women could hear the men bickering with one another again as they trudged away from the inn.

"Don't see what you're in such an all-fired rush to get home for all of a sudden..."

"Wouldn't know a hint if it dropped on your head, would you? Couldn't you tell the lass wanted to be alone with her young man?"

"Young man? You mean Dane? He went home with his da, oh, maybe two hours ago."

"Not him, the new fellow who was sitting with her."

"New fellow? I thought that was a lass. Wasn't it?"

"Eh... hard to say, hard to say. Coulda been. Don't mean little Louisa didn't want to be alone with her..."

"Well, that'll be a pretty pickle for our Dane, won't it?"

"Eh, depends, depends..."

Louisa, her face crimson, shut the door firmly and

latched it with a bit of wood on a hinge. "Well!" she said loudly as she walked back over to Dea's table, then seemed unable to think of what to say next so she flopped back down on her chair with a sharp huff of dismay and sat there blushing. They were now alone in the main room of the inn, aside from the old man snoring quietly to himself in the corner chair. Unless he was very good at impersonating the noise made by a hive of bees he was most definitely asleep; with Louisa's parents having gone to bed hours ago they were the only two people left awake in the whole building.

Dea picked idly at a bit of dirt under one of her claw-like nails. Eventually she said, "It's funny, I don't recall there being any sorceress in the version of the story *I* know."

"There's always got to be a wicked sorceress," Louisa said loftily, "if the story is going to be any good. Or sometimes a wizard, or something like that—but somebody magical and wicked, anyway. Otherwise how would bad things ever happen to the heroes and their ladies?"

Dea shrugged. "There's always life I suppose. It tends to provide more than enough excitement, the good and bad sort both, without the help of any wizards that I've ever noticed."

"Oh, in *real* life of course," Louisa said. "But not in *stories*."

Dea's eyes flicked up to meet Louisa's gaze and she raised an eyebrow.

Louisa's cheeks, which has just started to resume their normal peachy-pink color, flushed dark again. "Er, which doesn't make much sense when the story *was* your real life, I suppose..."

Dea chuckled. "It's all right. I got used to the whole 'passing into legend' thing a long time ago. It's something you have to come to terms with, if you're going to be a dragon."

"You really..." Louisa paused and chewed on her lip a moment, then continued in a hushed voice, "You really wanted—*want*—to become a dragon?"

"Of course!" Dea laughed. "It's not something that tends to happen to a person by accident, you know?"

"I don't see how I would," Louisa said waspishly. "Up until tonight all I knew about dragons was the regular sort of stories people tell about them burning villages and fighting knights. I never heard of dragons who are really faerie godmothers, or who used to be people, or who rescue princesses instead of kidnapping them."

"I'm sorry," Dea said. "I wasn't trying to make fun. Sometimes I forget not everyone has had as much experience with dragons as me."

Louisa sniffed but her stiff shoulders softened. "That's all right. I expect you've had many more interesting experiences than everybody in all of Styseville combined, traveling around like you do."

"You could have adventures too, if you want," Dea told her. "I suggest starting with the education because while a natural magical gift is all well and good, it can be dangerous without training, but once you've gotten a handle on your abilities—"

"My abilities!" Louisa exclaimed. "Now here, mistress, you listen: I'm just an ordinary girl, all right? I haven't got any magical abilities, and I certainly can't summon dragons — imaginary or otherwise! I'm sure you mean well, but you're making a mistake."

"I rarely make mistakes about dragons," Dea said.

"You did this time," Louisa said, her voice firm now. "I appreciate you trying to help us with our dragon problem, but really, what we need is a knight."

Dea shook her head. "This isn't the sort of dragon a knight can slay. At least not in the ordinary way. This is the sort of dragon that more often leads to witch-burning than dragon-slaying, and that's not the kind of solution you want—you least of all."

"Nonsense," Louisa said shrilly. Whatever spell Dea's words had cast on her had been broken by the interruption of the old men, and she was no longer listening. "Truly mistress, you've told an interesting tale, but it's not the first time I've heard someone too deep in their cups make impossible claims." She rose to her feet. "Unless you'd like more cider to wash your words down with, I think it's past time to call it a night."

Dea caught her wrist before she could move away. "Please, you really must believe me. The dragon is yours, and—"

"Fiddle-faddle," Louisa retorted, pulling free. "Now, the inn is closing. Do you wish a room for the night, or will you be moving on?" Her round face had gone hard and mullish and her eyes glittered stubbornly in the fading light of the fire.

Dea sighed. "I shall take a room, thank you," she said evenly. "I should hate to wander at night, with a dragon on the loose." Her gaze was pointed but Louisa ducked it and turned away.

"Follow me, mistress," Louisa said loftily, "I shall show you to your room."

"Thank you," Dea said again, her voice mild. She hefted her pack over one shoulder and followed the stiff-backed girl up a narrow set of stairs and down a hallway lit only by the candle Louisa carried. She proceeded Dea into the small bedroom and lit the taper on the table within.

"Will you need anything else tonight?" Louisa asked. There was distance in her tone and a challenge in her eyes, but Dea just shook her head. "Then I wish you pleasant dreams," Louisa said, and turned haughtily on her heel.

Dea let her leave without further protest. She put down her pack and looked around her temporary quarters. The room was small, with no furniture beside the bed with its straw-stuffed mattress and the rickety table that held a washbasin and pitcher in addition to the candle. There was a small un-paned window, its shutters open to bathe the room in moonlight that gave more light than the solitary candlestick. The dragon's apprentice sighed and paced a little, and looked out at the hazy half-moon that gleamed in the sky like a disapproving eye.

"It's not like I didn't try and tell her," Dea said tartly to the moon, and pulled the shutter closed to block the cold, pale light. She took off her boots and cloak and scarf and rolled herself into the hollow in the straw mattress that dozens of bodies had left before her. She didn't bother to undress; she doubted she would be in the bed very long. While the dragon did not visit Styesville every night, Dea was certain it would come on this one. There was no way that Louisa's dreams would not be filled with scales and flames after what she had learned tonight.

Dea's suspicions were not disappointed. Less than two hours after she'd closed her eyes she was awakened by the sound of people shrieking and the dull, heavy beat of wings against the air. Dea rose and pulled her boots back on, then arranged her scarf and cloak carefully to cover her scales. She did not hurry as she walked downstairs and out of the inn.

Outside all was in an uproar. People clad in nightshirts and untied boots milled around in a panic, all shouting at one another, many of them carrying vessels filled with water and others clutching tight-strung bows and fistfuls of arrows. Most of the archers were clustered around a knot of children, all of them too small yet to be of much help fighting fires, and most of the older ones holding wailing babies or squirming toddlers. The armed adults watched the skies with drawn faces and nocked arrows, as though ready to shoot down any clawed paw that reached for the little ones.

Dea snorted and clenched her lips tight so she would not laugh. It was cruel, she knew, but she could not help but find amusement in such a display of foolishness. As if any of their little hunting bows could hurt an actual dragon! Still, she had to admire their bravery, she told herself; how many times had she seen hardened soldiers flee from the shadows of a dragon's wing? These peasants were outmatched even by an imaginary dragon, but that hadn't stopped them trying to protect their homes and families from the beast riding the moonlit clouds overhead. She ought not to judge them so harshly. As Louisa had said, most people did not have her experience with dragons.

Reminded of the girl, Dea looked around for her now. She found Louisa by the village well, passing crockery and buckets down the line of villagers jostling around it. They tossed the contents of their jugs and jars on their homes, wetting the thatch and churning the dirt underfoot into a kind of muddy soup. Overhead the dragon swooped down close and roared.

Dea had to bite a knuckle to keep from objecting. She had heard all manner of dragon-roars in her life, but never had she heard one that sounded quite so much like a bear. If she had still required any evidence to convince her that this was a conjured beast and not an actual dragon, she had it now. As a creature summoned from Louisa's dreams, the dragon was constrained by the limits of her memories and imagination. While Louisa had never experienced the bone-shivering grumble of a dragon's bellow, she had doubtless heard a bear at least once or twice, so that was from where this dragon drew its voice.

Its size and ferocity came from stories. The beast's teeth and claws were well enough, long and sharp and seemingly made of silver, and its scales gleamed convincingly in the moonlight. Its stunted wingspan could never have lifted a creature of such girth however, and its tail thrashed in a manner that would have been decidedly inconvenient if its flight-path had been dependent on natural laws. Dea chuckled, as impressed as she was amused. Louisa certainly did have talent; all she lacked was education and scope. Dea hoped to offer her both, preferably before her marital jitters burned this little town down.

Just for the sake of being absolutely sure, she dug in her pouch and took out a bit of twisted wire that looked like something halfway between a jeweler's loop and a bracelet. It was made of strands of silver and bronze twisted together around a lens that looked like tinted glass but was in reality a thin-shaved scrap of dragon scale. Dea raised the loop to her eye and looked at the dragon through it. Her lips moved but whatever words she whispered were lost under the sounds of panicking villagers. Pale gems the size of ants—moonstones mainly—woven in the loop of wire glinted. So did the dragon when viewed through the lens of the scale. The beast looked like a tracery of itself made in ribbons of glittering pyrite and amber. Those ribbons all reached down to something on the ground: Louisa. When viewed through the scale she, too, looked like she was shot through with strands of light. Those strands pulsed, power flowing up them in heartbeat bulges to the dragon overhead.

Dea smirked and put the tool away.

The dragon roared twice more and unleashed a burst of rosy flame that crisped the edges of three cottages and made everyone below scream and duck. By the time the villagers had picked themselves out of the mud and re-gathered their wits, the dragon was gone. Dea ran for the edge of town and scrambled up the blacksmith's roof. From her perch there she could see the faint shadow of the beast flying away, its wings silent now though they still beat the air, or seemed to. The dragon flickered and faded, as though it were passing behind heavy clouds, and then was gone.

Dea smiled grimly and sat back against the slope of the roof, listening to the sounds of Styesville putting itself back in order. It took a little over an hour; clearly they had practice at visits from this dragon and had whittled the chaotic aftermath down to an efficient flutter. When she judged the last of the doors and shutters had been fastened, Dea jumped down from her roof and returned to the inn. She took care to walk in the deepest parts of the village's shadows; the sight of a scale-faced woman skulking around after the dragon's visit would raise ugly questions at the most, if not an outright mob, and Dea had no desire to become entangled in such unpleasantness.

When she entered the inn she found Louisa sweeping mud out the backdoor while a portly man who was surely her father collected the mugs left behind by the valiant defenders of the village. Dea stepped back into the corner to wait. Louisa's pink cheeks were pale and her shoulders shook. Her father chattered but Louisa made little reply beyond forced smiles and nervous giggles. Eventually he left, yawning, telling his daughter she could leave the rest of the mess for the morning.

"Yes, da," Louisa said. "I'll just finish this bit by the door first, 'fore it dries."

Dea waited until the sound of the innkeeper's footsteps faded then drew back her hood and stepped forward into the dim circle of light from the hearth's embers. Louisa yelped when she saw her, the broom falling to the floorboards with a clatter. A snort came from upstairs and Dea tensed, but no other sounds followed. She walked forward and picked up the broom, holding it out like an offering. Louisa hesitated, her round face wan and drawn, then finally wrapped trembling fingers around the handle.

"That was exciting," Dea said drily. "Are dragon raids always like that here?"

Louisa flinched. "At least no one was hurt," she said, defensively. "Nobody got burned or stolen or ate."

"People are among a dragon's least favorite food," Dea said. Her smile made it hard to tell whether or not she was joking; Louisa decided not to ask. "They much prefer talking to folk to eating them. More interesting that way, and they might as well eat a sheep or a salmon and save the people for gossiping with after the meal. Or during, if they have strong stomachs. Dragons aren't exactly dainty eaters, most of them."

Louisa relaxed a little at Dea's cheerful, casual tone, but she did not smile back.

"Frankly, I was impressed at how efficiently everyone handled things," Dea continued. "The line for water at the well, the archers watching the little ones—not that they needed to, but I suppose they wouldn't know that — the speed with which everything got cleaned up after and how readily everyone returned home rather than staying here 'til dawn to gossip... it was all very neatly done, really." Her gaze sharpened. "So was the dragon, for that matter. A very impressive creation, considering it was made by someone who's never seen such a beast before."

Louisa gulped. "But I didn't — "

"You did," Dea interrupted, not ungently. "I watched. I saw it, and I saw where it was anchored. The dragon is yours, Louisa."

"No."

"Yes," Dea insisted. "Come, sit down. We should talk."

Louisa continued to shake her head but she let Dea draw

her over to a table by the hearth and take the broom away again. Dea leaned it against the chimney and took a seat herself. She extended a hand palm-up on the table. After a moment, Louisa took it.

"It's time to stop lying to yourself," Dea told her. "I'm certainly not fooled and, at least after tonight, I don't think you are either."

Louisa looked down. She worried her lip between her teeth and said nothing.

"There's no sense blaming yourself," Dea pointed out. "You didn't conjure the dragon on purpose. No one could expect you to control a magic you didn't even know you possessed. You haven't been taught how to manage it, and that's not your fault. But you could learn."

Louisa said nothing for several minutes. She chewed on her lip and studied her empty palms.

Dea didn't rush her; just sat patiently and watched the crumbling embers in the hearth and the steady curl of smoke up the stone-and-plaster chimney.

"You really think I would do all right at that sort of thing? That sort of learning?"

"I think you would be *brilliant* at that sort of thing," Dea assured her. "Look what you did without any training at all, Louisa. Personally I look forward to seeing what you can do once you actually know what you're doing."

"And... and the dragon would go away from here when I did? There wouldn't be any more fires, or animals being stolen, or—or anything else?"

"None. Without you, there *is* no dragon."

Louisa thought about it for another minute. Then she asked, "What if I stayed here?"

"Well, then I think the dragon would get stronger and stronger the closer you get to that wedding you don't want." Dea's voice was soft but firm. "I think it quite likely that more than just some sheep would get hurt. Mayhap the groom, or even your parents since they're the ones who have put you in this position. Dragons," she added, "are honorable yes, but they do not have the same sense of morality that humans do—especially not imaginary dragons."

"Well." Louisa wiped her eyes briskly with the back of her hand. "Mayhap I don't want to marry Dane but he's a perfectly nice lad and he doesn't deserve being eaten by a dragon, even an imaginary one, and ma and da certainly don't, even if they do think a girl ought to be married for her own good." She took a deep breath, gathering herself together from stray bits and wisps of worries, then stood up.

"All right," she said. "Let me pack."

Dea smiled. "I think you're making a good decision."

Louisa nodded, not meeting her eyes. She had her lip between her teeth again and was worrying at it like a dog with a bone it wasn't convinced it really wanted but couldn't bear to let go.

"I think you'll enjoy the university," Dea told her. "And I'm sure you'll like Klarns. It's a colorful city and fond of celebrating—a bit *too* fond for my tastes sometimes," she added wryly. "I've spent too much time alone on the road and off studying with dragons to really enjoy big human festivals, but you seemed quite in your element here in the inn. It's just a guess, but I imagine you'll do just as well if not better in an even bigger, livelier crowd."

"It does get a bit dull here sometimes," Louisa admitted, then flinched. Her head came up with a jolt and she met Dea's eyes with with a wide, startled gaze. "Did—did you say *Klarns?* As in the Klarns that's on the other end of the *world?"*

"Not the whole world," Dea clarified. "Just this

continent. There are others, you know..." Seeing that her words didn't appear to be offering any comfort, she changed tack. "Yes, I mean that Klarns, but it's not a bad journey there this time of year. It'll get hotter as we go south, true, but that means no slogging through snow or sleet and I imagine any woman who can conjure an illusory dragon can learn how to make herself seem unappealing to the sort of insects who like to bite and sting. I can probably teach you some helpful tricks in that regard, if you like." Dea was trying hard to be encouraging; it wasn't something she got much practice at, spending time with dragons or by herself, but Louisa seemed to appreciate the effort if the watery smile she offered in return was any indication.

Dea continued in a voice as cheery as she could muster: "I've made the journey there several times. Admittedly I'm not very sociable, but I expect you'll be able to bear with me for a few months—and if I grow too tiresome, well there are always convoys and caravans with trade goods and performers and curious pilgrims heading to Klarns you could travel the rest of the way with instead without much difficulty. Less difficulty than traveling with a crotchety partial-dragon faerie godmother-in-training."

That earned her a weak laugh, much to Dea's relief; she had not known Louisa long but already she could tell that the innkeeper's daughter was by nature a cheerful person, and seeing her sorrowful had been uncomfortable. She wondered what Louisa's parents had been thinking when they had arranged her marriage, but of course it had probably been the same thing her own parents had thought so many years ago when they had locked her in that tower: that it would be for her own good in the end. Well, there was no full-fledged dragon here to rescue Louisa, but the Stylesville Inn was no impenetrable tower ringed with hungry beasts and a brambly hedge either. An apprentice dragon would do quite well, probably.

"You'll come?" Dea asked. "You'll give Klarns a try?"

Louisa shrugged. "It doesn't seem I've much of a choice."

"Of course you have," said Dea, suddenly firm. "You can go anywhere you like. I've been to a great many places, all over this continent and the others; all you have to do is tell me what sort of place you're looking for, what sort of thing you'd like to do with your life, and I'll offer as many possibilities as I can. The university is just a suggestion—"

"Not that," Louisa interrupted, flapping her hands as though Dea's words were pesky moths she could shoo away. "No, the university sounds—well, it sounds like something out of a faerie tale." She laughed. "Not something I ever thought in a hundred years that *I* would... no, I meant it doesn't seem as though I've a choice about leaving. I've got to go *somewhere*, so why not Klarns, I suppose?"

Dea shrugged. "You could stay," she pointed out. "Get used to your marriage with young Dane, learn to like—or at least live with—the idea. He seems a nice enough fellow. You could probably even manage to be happy, in a way. If you come to terms with the idea, you'll stop conjuring the dragon, and life here will go back to normal for everyone. I might even be able to teach you how to stop calling it on purpose, teach you how to suppress your gifts instead of master them. It's your choice what you do with your life. You don't *have* to leave."

Louisa looked around the room. It was low-ceilinged and plain with soot-stains above the hearth and splotches of assorted liquors and foodstuffs on the wooden boards of the floor. The doorway to the kitchen was covered by nothing more than a long sheet of cloth that bore the signs of much passage by someone whose hands were too full of food and drink to flick it aside. A narrow wooden stair led up to the second floor where they had the rooms for visitors. There was a faintly *agricultural* look to everything, not so much in that there was dirt or mud anywhere other than the floor but more in the feeling of the room; the people who ate here and drank here brought the wet smell of fresh-turned earth and musky goats in with them, and while the dirt could be swept out the smell—the *feeling*—lingered.

"I think I do," Louisa said quietly. She met Dea's eyes again. There were tear-streaks on her blotchy pink face but her eyes were clear. "I think it would be best for—for *everyone*."

"Probably," Dea agreed. "I'm sorry, for what it's worth. Sometimes home isn't."

"Do you miss yours ever?" Louisa asked. "Your—your castle?"

Dea blinked. "No," she said, after a moment's startled reflection. "To be honest it's been so long since I was there that I don't think of it as home anymore."

"Where is home then, for you?"

"With one of the dragons, I suppose?" Dea shrugged. "That or the road. I've been traveling for—oh, for longer than you've been alive, now. I like being on the move." She grinned. "I suppose it's the dragon in me: I don't like staying in one place too much, don't like being bored. I'd rather see something *new* than go back to somewhere that I know."

"I suppose you've found the right life, then."

"I think so," Dea agreed. "Which is good—there's not much *going back* once you've started down the draconian path." Her smile was crooked and full of more teeth than most people had. "It's so hard to explain the wings and scales in any other profession, too."

Louisa giggled then stopped, awed. "Do you—do you really have *wings*?"

"Not yet. Not really. Just sort of—the beginnings of wings. They're not good for much but getting in the way of the straps of my pack yet, honestly." Dea shrugged, then smirked. "I'm afraid I can't offer the traditional dragonback-flight to the distressed damsel," she teased, "but I can jump off very tall things without getting hurt so long as I take my shirt off first so that I can glide down on my stubby little skin-flaps, like a maple seed." She smiled and added wryly, "Mind you, doing so is a bit awkward right now because I'm still mostly mammalian in front; full dragons only have flat scales to expose which is why they don't bother wearing clothes to begin with." The warm blush on Louisa's cheeks made Dea curse herself silently; she *knew* the girl had taken a fancy to her, and here she was talking about her bosom.

Wanting to change the subject, she said quickly, "At any rate, may I offer you a bit of advice? Not from a dragon or a faerie godmother or an apprentice, but from a—from a former princess?" Louisa nodded, still looking very pink about the face. "Even if you don't want to say your farewells in person you should tell your parents that you're leaving. In a letter, perchance, if you'd rather not do it to their faces."

Louisa started, staring at Dea in shock. Dea sighed. She should probably explain about dragon-eyed insights, but perhaps not until the girl had had a few days to get used to some of the less strange aspects of Dea's current state of being halfway between species. For now she just said, "Sometimes farewells are easier when they're *not* spoken face-to-face. But you can still explain to them... well, whatever parts of it you want to explain." The smile she offered was rueful. "That's the one thing I wish I'd done differently when I left. I'm not sure it would have stopped the stories saying I was kidnapped, but it might have helped. And at least my parents wouldn't have worried so much. I do regret that, although never the leaving."

Louisa was very quiet for a long moment. "What do you think I should do?" she asked.

"I think you should write them a letter," Dea said, her voice grim. "I can play scribe and take dictation if you don't know how; your parents can get someone to read it to them if they can't do it themselves. I think it's a lot safer to say goodbye in a letter. If nobody knows you're leaving until you're a few miles down the road, it's much harder for them to stop you."

"They're not going to stop me," Louisa protested. "Not once I explain."

"I think they will try." Dea caught her eyes and held them coldly with her slit-pupiled green gaze. Louisa would have shivered but she couldn't move. "I think that telling them you're leaving yourself, and why, even a little bit of why, is an idea that you will regret. But it's up to you."

She blinked, and Louisa—freed from her stare—took a shaky breath. "They're my *parents*. I'm going to tell them."

"Suit yourself," Dea said. "In that case, I'm going back to bed. You can take the night to pack, and tell your parents in the morning—if you haven't changed your mind by then—and if all goes well, we can leave early and start the journey to Klarns, or wherever you choose to go."

"I'm going to go to Klarns," Louisa said, "and my parents are going to wave goodbye when I do."

Dea's crooked smile said plainly that she doubted it, but she held her tongue still and kept her words behind her teeth. Everyone deserved to make their own choices—and mistakes—and part of being a dragon was in letting people do so. Part of being a faerie godmother meant offering only the help that was *asked* for; you could tell a person that you knew better than them, but you mustn't *force* it.

She left Louisa and returned to her small rented room. Dawn was still a few hours late, but after the dragon's nighttime visit Dea expected most of the village to sleep late. This time she undressed properly and settled in on the rustling straw mattress for a proper rest. She did not snore as she slept, but she did whistle a bit, like a small kettle left on the hearth to simmer.

Morning came suddenly with shouts and the sharp, scattering sound of breaking crockery. Dea sat up with a sigh and started to dress. *Three guesses what precipitated that uproar,* she thought cynically, and finger-combed her hair out of habit before she pulled her hood down and her scarf up to hide her scale-spotted face. Then she walked downstairs and, finding no one in the long low-ceilinged room (although there was a small puddle of milk cluttered with bits of broken clay on the floor near the kitchen curtain), she hitched her pack higher on her shoulders and went out the front door.

It didn't take long to find Louisa; all Dea had to do was follow the shouting. The girl had been dragged to the center of town by what were surely her parents. They looked worried, stricken. They each held Louisa by one arm while they spoke fearfully to what had to be a priest of some sort. (Dea had given up years ago on keeping track of human religions which seemed to her to be constantly splintering, restructuring, and re-naming themselves; it was enough to know that he was a religious official without knowing what sort of god or gods he served.) A crowd had gathered; it probably didn't take much to summon a crowd in Styesville. If it was anything like all the other small villages that Dea had encountered on her journeys then there wouldn't be much offered here in the way of entertainment other than personal drama and gossip about one's neighbors, so anything out of the ordinary attracted everyone's attention. She wouldn't be surprised to find the whole town come to watch the show if it went on another few minutes.

"I am not under any spell!" Louisa protested loudly. It sounded like something she'd already said a great many times today. "I told you, I'm the one casting the—well, it's not a spell exactly I suppose since I don't know how to cast it on purpose, but I am the one imagining the dragon!"

"My dear, dear child!" The priest was a pudgy fellow with wispy streaks of hair combed across a balding scalp. His pasty skin held the faded tan of a man who had once spent most of his time outdoors but now lived a sedentary, indoor life. He wore a robe woven of high-quality cloth that had been dyed a soft, almost sickly blue, like the sky right before a summer thunderstorm. It was edged with complicated embroidered patterns, probably sigils that held some significance to practitioners of whatever beliefs were common in Styesville. His eyes were watery green with fat, swollen pouches underneath. The way he flapped his hands made Dea think of the crows from yesterday, but of course while crows were coarse and mean they were also clever, and Dea didn't think anybody who used phrases like "my dear child" in earnest deserved the benefit of the doubt when it came to an assessment of their intelligence.

His next words did nothing to suggest she should change her mind: "No need to upset yourself; we'll sort this out don't you worry, lass. Just you hush yourself now and let your elders talk, eh?"

"You don't understand, I have to leave or else—"

"Hush, my dear! Just you be patient a moment and we'll have everything worked out." He waved his hand and two fellows with muscled arms and placid expressions that put one in mind of oxen more than anything else walked over and, not ungently, took hold of Louisa's arms while the priest drew her parents aside for a whispered conversation. Dea crept closer to listen, her sharp ears easily picking out his hurried words:

"We must have the wedding at once, I think—dragon or no dragon."

"The wedding?" Louisa's mother gasped. "Are you mad? My lass is sick or possessed; she needs medicine or an exorcism, not a marriage!"

"Ah!" said the priest, tapping his nose in a manner that he doubtless thought made him look sage, "The wedding will fix all of that, I think! Oh yes. It seems to me more likely that the poor girl is merely suffering jitters due to the delay of her marriage, and what she needs is—*ahem*—the guiding hand of a husband."

Louisa's father didn't look convinced but her mother was already nodding along, although with little enthusiasm. "I suppose you would know best..." the innkeeper said hesitantly.

"Quite, yes! This is the sort of thing I'm here for, my son; have faith in me and I'll see it all settled neat as you could want. We'll have to rush I'm afraid, no time to wait for ceremony if the dragon has already begun to ensorcel her. Go and fetch the lad and his family," he told Louisa's father confidently, "and I'll see to it that everything else needful is prepared."

Dea rolled her dragon-bright eyes and slipped away as a crowd started to gather in earnest.

The village was too small to muster an actual temple but there were rough wooden benches arranged in a semi-circle outside facing a stone altar on which flowers were currently being quickly piled by some of the village children. Louisa's mother waited at the door of the priest's cottage with one of the ox-like men; half offering a mother's support to a nervous bride and half acting as guard to keep the bewitched girl from escaping.

Dea ignored the cluster of activity around the door and benches and walked around to the back of the small building (noting with some approval that the shingles on this roof were scorched just like the rest of the town) where a high window let in light and air. It wasn't hard for a woman with dragon claws to climb the wooden slats and raise herself over the sill so she could see inside. She didn't even need to unwrap her wing-stubs for such a little height as this. Cottages, unsurprisingly, were easier to breech than towers, perhaps explaining why dragons generally preferred princesses to peasants: they liked a challenge. Being but an apprentice-dragon, Dea thought that starting with a cottage seemed an entirely sensible course of action, even if it wasn't likely to result in the sort of story her dragon-kin liked to listen to. Besides, she could hardly abandon Louisa now, regardless of the bardic potential her rescue did or did not offer.

Louisa for her part was curled in a corner with her hands pressed over her face, weeping. Nothing about her looked like someone expecting a rescue, and Dea's heart felt squeezed suddenly inside her scale-dusted chest at the thought Louisa had believed herself so readily abandoned.

Dea's sharp hiss carried like a shout over Louisa's muffled tears. Louisa started, curls thrashing, and looked around the tidy room before she spotted Dea in the window's opening. She gasped and scrambled to her feet.

"You were right!" she sobbed. The floor inside was built-up enough that the shorter woman could reach the windowsill without climbing, although only with her fingertips. She brushed them over Dea's thick nail-claws; she was trembling. "I should have listened!"

"Even I don't take my own advice all the time," Dea said drily. "Please stop crying. It's not as bad as all that."

"Yes it is!" Louisa protested. "You don't understand. They're going to come and get me in a few minutes and then I'll have to marry Dane. No more delays on account of the dragon. They think I'm under a spell, and that will cure it. Ha!" she said bitterly. "Now I'll never be able to stop the dragon and it will come and burn everything down and people will die and it will be all my fault, because I should have listened!"

"Hush," growled Dea. "I'm not dragon enough yet to enjoy such levels of melodrama. Now get out of the way; I don't want to land on you."

"Land on—?" Louisa gulped and scrambled backwards as Dea hoisted herself up and through the window. She dropped lightly to the floor, the *thud* of the wooden boards underfoot almost drowned-out by the chatter outside.

"I couldn't very well boost you up from out there, could I?" she asked. "Now hurry—before they come to fetch you for the wedding. You *do* still *want* to leave, don't you?"

"Of course!" Louisa said. "More than ever! But—you can't possibly lift me, a skinny thing like you..."

"I'm stronger than I look," Dea said firmly. She knelt by the window and cupped her hands together to make a step. "Now come on, stop fussing."

Louisa fluttered but did as she was told, still sniffling a little, and Dea gave a grunt as she heaved with hands and knees. Louisa squeaked and scrambled over the sill. There was a *thump* and another, louder squeak as she hit the ground outside. Dea dug her nails into the soft wood of the windowsill and followed, easily leaping over the crumpled form of the other woman and landing nimbly on her feet. She reached down and tugged Louisa upright.

"Well come on then, we don't have time to waste. Did you finish packing last night?"

"Packing?" Louisa repeated, sounding a little breathless. "Aye, but I didn't bring anything with me when they dragged me away to see Brother Bauik." When Dea simply nodded and tugged her in the direction she'd come from Louisa paled and drew back. "We're not—not going back home, surely? To the inn, I mean?"

"Unless you want to walk all the way to Klarns in nothing but that dress we are," Dea replied calmly. "Come along, and don't worry so. Everyone else is coming *here*, so there won't be anyone to see us *there*. We'll nip in and grab your things and be on the road before they've figured out you've gone—with any luck."

Dea did not mention that dragons do not, as a rule, believe in luck and certainly do not approve of relying on it. When they turned the corner of the cottage only to come face-to-face with a crowd of busy villagers including none other than the priest himself and the young strawberry-haired man who thought he was supposed to be marrying Louisa in a few minutes, she remembered why.

Fortunately the filthy oath she snarled was draconian and none of the inhabitants of Styesville spoke that archaic tongue, or she would doubtless have been greeted with more outrage than surprise. As it was, the attention of the startled villagers focused first on Louisa. It consisted at first mainly of cries expressing their surprise that she had escaped (not that they used such a word; that would imply she had been a prisoner, and people who are forcing others to act "for their own good" rarely see it as a prison, as Dea knew all too well). The first person to really take note of *her* was the priest. When his eyes bulged and the veins in his face swelled Dea realized that in her scramble in and out of the window her hood had fallen. She reached to pull it back over her head but stopped when she realized it was already too late: the priest was pointing a shaking hand at her.

"D-d-d-dragon!" he shrieked.

Louisa moaned and spun to look behind her; Dea, who knew very well what the priest was pointing at, did not. The other villagers in Styesville did not have to turn, because she was standing right in front of them. Suddenly a runaway bride was no longer the most interesting thing to stare at. Dea sighed and stared back, refusing to be made to feel abashed for her scales. She had chosen them of her own free will, and no scandalized villagers were going to make her feel ashamed over that choice now. She fixed the priest with a slit-eyed stare. He yelped and ducked behind a tall man who had flour dust up to his elbows; the miller no doubt, unless he was the village's baker. Whoever he was, he did not look pleased about being the priest's shield, and his face turned almost as pasty as his hands.

"That can't be the dragon," someone protested. "That looks like a... girl?"

"The fiend has taken human shape to lure our poor lass into its clutches!" the priest cried, clinging to the miller. "But see, by the holy light of day it cannot hide its true nature!"

"Don't be ridiculous," Dea said, without much hope that anybody would listen. "I look like this in any light. And I'm not a dragon." *Not yet anyway*, she added silently. *And maybe not ever, if you lot have your way*.

Louisa, cheeks bright pink, turned back to face her fellow villagers. "She certainly is not! I told you, there isn't a dragon—not a real one, anyway! It's all my imagination!"

"It's true," Dea said, raising her voice to be heard although she wasn't sure why she was bothering. "That is why it is important that Louisa go somewhere she can learn how to use her talents properly, deliberately, instead of—"

"Lies!" the priest shrieked. "Stop your ears, my brethren! Do not let it ensnare any more of you!"

Dea scowled; anyone who tried to win an argument by silencing the other party was, as far as she was concerned, not worth listening to, but several villagers shrank back obediently and if they didn't actually clap their hands to their ears they did avert their eyes and shuffle their feet awkwardly, torn between wanting to do as they were told and not wanting to miss a moment of the scandal. Louisa's mother was weeping openly while two other women supported her on either side. The prospective groom shoved his way to the front of the crowd.

"Louisa, come away!" said Dane. He was sweating nervously. "Before it—before it hurts you. Please."

"She's not going to hurt me!" Louisa snapped. "She's here to help."

"Help with what?" someone asked.

"With... with getting rid of my dragon," Louisa said, dropping her gaze evasively. "And... not getting married."

"Not married?"

"I told you she was bewitched!"

"It's not enough for the dragon to steal our sheep, it wants our women as well!"

"Poor Louisa! We mustn't let it harm her!"

"Oh, poppycock," Dea muttered.

"If it's in people-shape now, does that mean it will be easier to kill?"

"That's how it always works with monsters in the stories!"

"Somebody grab it!"

"You grab it."

Louisa stamped her foot. "Nobody is grabbing anybody! You settle down right now, Jack Hempswitch!"

One bushy-bearded man had the decency to look ashamed, but the rest of the crowd was undaunted by Louisa's scolding, and from the look of things more than a few had started to discuss strategy. Dea suspected that it would come to violence in a few moments.

"If we burn the dragon it can't burn us anymore!" one villager screamed, proving her right.

There was a sudden surge of movement as the crowd

reached forward, ignoring Dane's frail cry of, "But Louisa! Don't hurt her!" Anger twisted their faces into ugly masks but at least, having been preparing for a wedding, none of them were armed with anything more dangerous than flower-garlands and belt-knives.

Dea raised her hands and they almost fell over one another to stop. Only the priest still tried to push forward, but because he was still tucked behind the solid miller, he didn't go far. "Don't let it scare you!" he yelped. "It can't hurt you when it's in human form! Our faith will guard us!"

"I don't want to hurt any of you," Dea snapped, "but if you persist in this—this *nonsense* I may be forced to, and I'd rather not do that. Now, all you have to do is let Mistress Louisa here decide what she wants to do with her *own* life—as I believe she has tried to explain to you several times already this morning—and no one will have to do anything rash, you *or* me."

"It was you who was rash coming here, dragon!" Dea almost expected the priest to start frothing at the mouth, but he didn't even spit as he shouted, showing more self-possession than most of his ilk that she'd encountered in her travels. "Now we have you where we want you! Now we can—"

"Dea isn't the dragon!" Louisa yelled. Everybody went silent, gaping at her. Her plump cheeks were flushed bright red. It seemed no one—at least no one like her—had ever interrupted the priest before. He gaped like a fish while everyone else stared. Louisa pushed on, refusing to let her embarrassment silence her: "I am! Or at least, I'm why it's coming here. And I don't want any of you to get hurt, and I'm sorry things got burned but I didn't mean it, and I didn't even know I was doing it, but I don't want to do it anymore." She turned to face Dane and her voice dropped from shouting to sorrowful. "I don't want to marry you either. I do like you, I just—I don't want to marry you. I'm sorry. That's part of why I have to go, and it's not your fault either, and I'm sorry. And ma, pa... I should have spoken up sooner. I'm sorry. That part's my fault, for sure. Maybe after I learn how to... how to do or *not* do whatever this is I can do, maybe—"

"You are *not* leaving!" Louisa's mother, her face as red with outrage as her daughter's was with shame, drew herself up. "You aren't going anywhere except over to that altar! Everything will look better once you're wed and this silly curse is broken!" She planted her hands on her hips. "Now I won't hear any more nonsense out of you, young lady!"

"Mother! You need to listen to me!"

"Don't talk to your mother in that tone of voice."

"Pa, don't you start now. Don't you see—"

"I see you've been dragon-addled, my girl, but we'll take care of that *and* this beastie..."

When the villagers, muttering darkly—some in the back of the crowd who felt themselves safe were shouting, but those whom Dea could look in the eye merely muttered—started forward again, Dea decided it was time to stop being polite. "That's enough," she snapped. Her green eyes glittered. "No one is getting married today and nobody has been cursed and nobody is going to be breaking any curses—or breaking or burning anything *else*, either. I am a faerie godmother and I will not put up with this sort of thing." Dea glared, although she knew that statements like that were a *lot* more impressive when issued by a creature that was over twelve feet tall and had wings the size of the sun. The mouths full of razor-sharp, swordblade-long teeth probably didn't hurt either.

"A faerie godmother?" somebody actually laughed, nervously.

"Louisa, you listen to me—"

"No." That was Dane, looking pale. "If'n she doesn't want to be married, we won't be married."

"Now son, you just think a moment—"

"Da, she said she doesn't want to. That's the end of it."

"It is not! The girl is cursed, and we can cure her!" The priest was using the miller's solid shoulder as a springboard now, lifting his balding crown above the crowd in little hops and jumps. "All we have to do is kill the dragon! We'll free the girl and our town in one blow—"

"It will take more than one." Dea's voice was a growl, the sort of growl that was heard by children waking in the dead of night when they know there's a monster under their bed; the sort of growl that is heard in the heart rather than through the ears; the sort of growl, in short, that people only hear when they face dragons. It sent a deep, primal shudder through the crowd—or at least through those parts of it that had more sense than faith.

"Then we'll keep hacking until you're dead, foul beast!" the priest shouted. "Onward, brethren!"

Nobody charged; instead there was a reluctant shuffle that moved sideways more than it did forward. The priest's already red face reddened further; the veins on the side of his head bulged and throbbed like a clogged hose.

Dea sighed and decided she ought to do something about the man before he talked someone else into getting hurt. "I said hold. Louisa has made her decision, so this discussion is at an end."

"You have no say here—"

"I rather think I do." Dea took a deep breath and held it; when she breathed out she did it like a bellows, all in one long gust of blisteringly hot air. The villagers in front of her shrieked, flailed, and fled. Even bold Dane waited for only one worried look at Louisa before he joined the others and ran. Louisa's parents were nowhere to be seen when the crowd was gone, nor was the priest. The sound of slamming doors, wailing voices, and shattering pottery as people tripped over their desperate fire-prevention piles filled the small village of Styesville.

Eventually everything was quiet save for one lone pig snuffling happily in something wet and mucky nearby. Dea took another deep breath and waved a hand in front of her face. "Phew!" she said. "That always stings!" She was sure she felt blisters rising but when she prodded the skin around her lips with exploratory fingers she couldn't find any. That didn't make her scalded flesh feel any better, though, and she couldn't help but ask, "Would it be bad form, do you suppose, if I got something to drink while you were collecting your things? I'd leave proper coin for it, of course..."

Louisa was staring at her, blue eyes wide and round face ashen. She was pressed against the wall of the priest's cottage, her hands fisted in her skirts. "You... I didn't know you could breathe fire," she said in a voice like a squeak.

"I can't," Dea replied. "That wasn't fire. That was just... *heat*."

"It was very hot heat."

Louisa sounded as shaken as she looked. Dea shrugged. "Well, some day it will be fire. Let's just be glad that for today, heat was enough. And let's hurry so we can be gone before anyone finds their courage again, eh?"

Paling even more, Louisa nodded. She led the way to the inn at a trot, Dea lagging behind so she could look around for trouble. She did pour herself another tankard of cider while Louisa trotted upstairs to fetch a tightly-knotted bundle and a warm cloak of her own. Unlike Dea she tied hers back over her shoulders; neither woman bothered to put their hoods up now. There was no point trying to hide, and the spring morning was rapidly warming.

The two women moved out, but Louisa hesitated on the threshold of the inn. She looked around, hope kindling in her blue eyes, but no one came forward to say farewell. All the doors around them were closed, the windows empty, and the streets barren of anything that walked on two legs. That did nothing to abate the sense of watchfulness that filled Styesville and made the hair stand up on the back of Dea's neck; her scales itched. The village was still and nearly silent, but she imagined eyes pressed to every crack and peeking out from the corner of every window. Dea crossed her arms to keep herself from fidgeting. Louisa had to do this at her own speed, and Dea knew that leaving home was no easy thing even after you had realized that there was no good way to stay.

Louisa took a step outside and wavered.

"Ready to go?" Dea asked gently.

Louisa took a deep breath. "You're sure the dragon will leave when I do?"

"Both the dragon and the dragon-faced girl," Dea said with a gentle smile.

"All right." Louisa nodded. She had started crying again at some point and now she dashed the tears from her face with a rough swipe of her open palm. "All right, I'm ready."

They started down the road slowly, Louisa glancing over her shoulder every few steps while Dea tried to ignore the feeling of eyes fixed on her back. Her skin prickled like someone had dribbled ice between the stubby wings concealed by her long cloak and heavy pack. She couldn't wait to pass out of sight of Styesville, but forced herself to walk slowly so as not to hurry her new companion.

When they crossed into the shadows of the southern forest a lark began to sing. A tiny smile stole over Louisa's tear-blotched face. She glanced sideways at Dea and asked shyly, "Are you *really* the Princess Aldeaim?"

Dea nodded. "Once upon a time."

Louisa thought for a minute, then grinned. "Well, you look quite well for your age, even if you *do* have scales."

"Perks of the job," Dea retorted. "Just wait until I start growing the tail..."

Fin

About the Author

Nicky was making up stories before she could write, acting them out with her handmade paper dolls or assorted action figures, usually with her little brother's amiable assistance. Once she mastered writing implements she turned her efforts toward both prose and pictures and is a fan of storytelling in all media, especially novels and comic books, and the only thing she likes more than telling people about things they should read is writing (or drawing) them herself. Of course, if she could stop her cat helping her type she'd probably make more headway...

Made in the USA
Coppell, TX
17 November 2020